the Littlest Witch

BIANCA PITZORNO

ILLUSTRATED BY MARK BEECH

TRANSLATION BY LAURA WATKINSON

Wanda

Imelda

Tabitha

Cassandra

Helena

Emilia

the
littlest
witch

CATNIP BOOKS
Published by Catnip Publishing Ltd.
320 City Road
London EC1V 2NZ

This edition published 2018
1 3 5 7 9 8 6 4 2

ISBN 978-1-910-61117-3

www.catnippublishing.co.uk

Printed and bound by CPI Group (UK) Ltd, Croydon, CR0 4YY

Sibylla

Zac

Diomira

Mephisto

Shut-Up

Alfonso

CONTENTS

The Essential Prologue

A smug little smirk flickered across Alfonso Terribile's lips. Rudely slumped in the lawyer's armchair, he was listening to the reading of his Great-Uncle Sempronio's will, who had passed away the week before from a fatal case of indigestion caused by eating too much fried fish.

Finally, thought Alfonso with satisfaction, *the ancient mummy has popped his clogs!*

Having read just these few lines, my dear readers, you will probably already have worked out that:

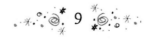

a. Great-Uncle Sempronio, when he was alive, had been very rich indeed and, upon his death, he had left a lot of money.
b. Alfonso Terribile was his only heir.
c. Alfonso was a heartless great-nephew who was incredibly selfish and money-grabbing.

What you couldn't have guessed though – but I'll tell you now and you'll have to trust me – is that Alfonso was also a most unattractive young man, with pimples all over his face, a weak chin, and crooked teeth that were turning green because they hadn't been brushed for so long. His greasy hair was full of dandruff, his ears were filthy and there was a black line around the collar of his shirt.

He was also very lazy and had never even contemplated thinking about the idea of work. *After all*, he always said to himself, *sooner or later I'll get my inheritance from*

Great-Uncle Sempronio!

As for Great-Uncle Sempronio – to put your minds at ease, because I'm sure you have a soft spot for old people – I will tell you that, well, yes, he was dead, but it happened at the age of ninety-nine, after he'd enjoyed a long life with all his many millions, and having such an unpleasant great-nephew had never bothered him for a moment.

Everyone expected all of the dearly departed's wealth to pass into the hands of his sole heir, and that was indeed what the solicitor was saying as he read the will in his monotonous voice. In fact, his voice was so slow and boring that Alfonso, sure that he already knew how the story was going to end, had almost nodded off. But then a line of the will hit him like a cold shower, making him leap up out of the chair.

'Whaaat??!!' spluttered the young man, gaping and opening his eyes wide.

Patiently, the solicitor reread the last paragraph: '*My only great-nephew, Alfonso Terribile, will take possession of my entire fortune one year and one month after my death, on one condition: that by that date he has married a witch.*'

'But this is madness!' yelled Alfonso. 'It has to be a joke, right? A witch? What century are we living in? Even little children know there's no such thing as witches these days!'

'Please calm down, sir, and allow me to continue reading,' said the solicitor calmly, and he went back to reading the will. '*I am aware that my great-nephew will think this condition absurd and will claim that witches no longer exist. But they most certainly do exist. You just have to know how to recognise them. I am quite an expert in this matter, in fact, as I was very happily married to my Prunisinda for many years, and she was a true witch through and through.*'

'Great-Aunt Prunisinda was a witch?!' exclaimed Alfonso, who had only the vaguest memory of Great-Uncle Sempronio's wife, a chubby and cheerful woman who had passed away more than twenty years earlier.

'*We were so happy together, in fact,*' the solicitor continued reading, '*that I would like to ensure the same happiness for my heir. So he must put his wits to work. Find a young witch. Woo her and wed her. If he has not succeeded within one year and one month of my death, then he is out of luck. My fortune will pass to the person or persons who are mentioned inside this sealed envelope, which may not be opened until that date comes. Until then, the solicitor must keep the envelope in his safe.*'

'This is insane!' Alfonso puffed and panted, feeling quite stunned. 'Find a witch? Woo a witch? Convince her to marry me?! But . . . that's impossible!'

However, Great-Uncle Sempronio's many millions – fifty of them, to be precise – were too tempting for him to give up just like that. Alfonso Terribile was going to do whatever it took to satisfy the conditions of his great-uncle's will.

The Real Story Begins – and the Main Characters Appear

Two days later, in the same city, at around ten o'clock in the morning, two cars stood waiting outside a maternity clinic. One was a yellow taxi with a driver. The other was an old Jeep of some indefinable colour, all bashed and dented, with no one inside.

The door of the clinic opened and a small group of people came out: an old man with a big grey beard, two teenage girls, an elegant gentleman carrying two big suitcases, and a beautiful woman in a fur coat, holding a bundle of blue blankets.

The bundle contained a new-born baby, who
had just been given the name of Sibylla. The
others were her parents, her grandpa on her
father's side, and her sisters Wanda and Imelda.

Sibylla's mother was a famous actress, who had
interrupted a successful theatrical tour specially
to give birth to her. Now she was about to go
back on tour with her husband, who was also

her manager. So the taxi had been called to take them to the airport. Sibylla, on the other hand, was going home to wait for their return, in the care of her sisters and grandpa.

'Let's hope her hair will have started growing by the time we get back,' said her mother, stroking the baby's bald head in farewell. 'I'm so curious to find out if she'll have blonde or brown hair.'

'Brown, I think. Look at those big brown eyes!' her dad said fondly.

'No, I say blonde. When babies are born bald, they usually turn out blonde,' her mum said.

It was an old competition between the two of them. She was a blonde, while he was brown-haired, and they were both very keen to leave their mark on their offspring. Their six daughters so far, however, had divided exactly down the middle: three on the dark-haired side (one curly, one straight and one wavy), and the other three on the blonde side (one wavy, one curly and one straight).

And now little Sibylla, the latest arrival, had the power to tip the balance as soon as her first hair sprouted.

Two hours later, the plane rose into the sky, carrying the girls' parents towards a distant theatre in Stockholm. The Jeep, driven by their grandpa, had already taken the three sisters back to the shabby little house in the suburbs where the other four girls and Diomira were waiting. Diomira was their nanny and housekeeper. In truth, she was more interested in crosswords than housework though.

'But she's absolutely marvellous with babies,' their mother had told the journalists who were waiting at the airport to interview her. 'So we can leave with a clear conscience, knowing that Sibylla is in such good hands.'

The Zeps

Although Diomira was very good with little children, she'd never had any of her own. She was unmarried and had worked in the Zep household (yes, Zep – that was the family's surname) for about sixteen years. It was Diomira who had raised all the sisters, both the blondes and the brunettes.

But her darling, her absolute favourite child, was not a member of the Zep family. He was the orphan son of her late sister Ermelinda, and Diomira had taken care of him before becoming

Wanda's nanny.

Her beloved nephew was called Zaccaria, but most people knew him as Zac. He worked in the reading room at the local library.

An older lady at the library was in charge of the lending desk, but Zac was a lot nicer than her, so Cassandra and Tabitha preferred to sit in the reading room, rather than taking their books home.

They also liked the library because it was wonderfully calm, unlike their home, where it was impossible to find a quiet corner to read in peace. Part of the problem was those two little nuisances, Emilia and Helena, who were only six and seven years old and kept interrupting, jabbing their sticky, chocolate-covered fingers at the page and yelling 'What does that say?' or 'Why aren't there any pictures in this book?'

Then Emilia would claim that she wanted to 'read' with one of her big sisters.

She was only in the baby class at school though, so she took an eternity to read anything. By the time she'd reached the second line, her big sister was ready to turn the page, but Emilia expected her to wait, even if her sister was dying to find out if the bad guy had buried his knife:

a. in the hero's back,

b. in some other criminal's chest,

c. in a loaf of bread,

or

d. in a table top at the pub.

In short, reading at home was a trial. So the library, where there was also a nice little courtyard for sitting outside when the weather was good, was much better.

Tabitha and Cassandra, as you'll probably have realised, were the third and fourth Zep sisters. Tabitha was ten and Cassandra was nine, but they looked like twins, with their heads full of curls, even though Cassandra's hair was blonde and Tabitha's was brown.

Helena was the last sister but one, and Emilia was the baby of the family (until Sibylla came along, of course). They both had straight hair. Helena's hair was as dark as a little girl from China's and Emilia's was as blonde as the blondest Swedish girl's.

So now you've met all the family, except for Mephisto the cat and Shut-up the parrot.

Their grandpa's name was Lindoro, by the way. That's right. Lindoro Zep. What? You don't think that sounds much like a grandfather's name? Well, honestly, that really is what he was called.

Sibylla Has a Bath

Wanda, the eldest of the sisters, felt very responsible for Sibylla. So she decided to help Diomira to give her new little sister her first bath.

'Here's how we'll do it: I'll hold her and you can soap her up,' Wanda said when the tub was ready and the water was at the right temperature.

'No. You soap her and I'll hold her,' replied Diomira. 'If she slips out of your hands and goes under the water, she could drown, and what will we tell your mother when she gets home?'

Upset at this lack of confidence in her, Wanda grumpily began to rub soap on Sibylla's bald head, as the baby splashed happily in the warm water.

'No! Not like that!' barked Diomira. 'Can't you see you're getting soap in her eyes? Like this!' To show Wanda how to do it, she reached out her right hand and snatched the soap. But Sibylla slipped from her left hand, falling into the water.

'Oh no! She's going under! Grab her!' cried Imelda, who was assisting with the warm towels.

'She's drowning! She's drowning! Save her!' squealed Emilia and Helena excitedly.

But Sibylla didn't go under. She calmly stayed there, floating on the surface, lazily stretching her arms and legs and gazing up at the ceiling with her big brown eyes.

'She's swimming!' Cassandra said in amazement. 'She's only a tiny baby, but she knows how to swim!'

'No. It's not swimming. More like floating,' Tabitha pointed out.

They called in their grandpa to take a look at the strange phenomenon. To make absolutely certain there was no mistake, they filled the big bathtub up to the brim and put the baby in the deeper water.

There could be no doubt about it. Without anyone holding her, without any support to keep her on the surface of the water, Sibylla was FLOATING!!!

Like a rubber duck, like a lifebelt, like a water lily. She did not sink. When they gently pressed down on her tummy, she went under for a second before popping straight back up, as if she were full of air, or lighter than water.

'But she weighs four and a half kilos,' muttered Diomira, lifting her off the scales. 'That's a perfectly normal weight for a week-old baby. So why do other babies sink, and she doesn't?'

They called the doctor, but he wasn't able to explain the peculiar phenomenon either.

'The little one seems as fit as a fiddle,' he murmured, perplexed, as he watched her splashing about in the tub.

'You can say that again!' replied Grandpa, who was very proud of Sibylla's amazing feat.

So, in fact, her floating wasn't a problem after all. Quite the opposite! It meant that the bathing ceremony was no longer a worry for Diomira. She gladly allowed the older girls to help her and, one day when she didn't want to leave a particularly tricky crossword half-finished, she even let Cassandra and Tabitha give the baby a bath – all on their own.

A Stranger in the Library

Over the course of the next few days, Zac had his hands full searching the library for all the science books that the two middle Zep sisters had requested.

Cassandra and Tabitha had made up their minds to find out all about the laws of physics, and in particular why certain objects float and why others sink. Reading one book after another, they learned many, many interesting facts. However, according to all the authors, a baby in water will either swim or drown. Not one single scientist even briefly mentioned what had happened to Sibylla.

In the meantime, however, something rather unpleasant had occurred at the library.

For a number of days now, Tabitha and Cassandra had found their favourite table occupied by a reader they'd never seen before.

It was a large table and the two sisters could have squeezed themselves into their usual spots, but they chose instead to take themselves and their books as far away as possible.

'I think you're right to be suspicious,' said Zac, who hadn't failed to notice their move. 'He seems a bit bonkers, to be honest. He's been coming in here for a week now, and do you know what kind of books he keeps asking for? Ones about black magic! He even insisted that I bring up some mouldy old tomes from the basement, which I'd put aside to be repaired!'

The two girls just laughed. Black magic? In

this century?! And he wasn't even particularly ancient – he looked like he was in his twenties.

'Actually,' said Cassandra, 'that's not why we don't want to get too close to him. You know, he doesn't look like he's ever seen a bottle of shampoo. Have you noticed how greasy his hair is? And the dandruff!'

'And he's got spots all over his chin. He keeps popping them with his pencil. Bleurgh!' added Tabitha.

'His breath isn't exactly fresh either. Have you seen his teeth? Looks like there's moss growing on them,' Cassandra concluded.

'I'm sorry,' replied Zac, 'I can't ban him from the library for that. But next time he requests a book, maybe I'll take him a guide to personal hygiene as well.'

And that's exactly what he did. But the stranger was so buried in his books on black magic that he didn't even notice.

Shut-up Speaks

Little Emilia and Helena were itching to have a go at supervising Sibylla's bath time too.

Diomira had forbidden it though, so they decided they'd give the parrot a bath instead.

The Zeps' parrot was a beautiful bird that the sisters had given to their grandpa for his birthday, three years earlier. The man at the pet shop had guaranteed that the bird was a talking parrot, and for that reason he had been very expensive. Imelda, who'd gone to collect the bird, also swore that she'd clearly heard him saying a number of different sentences when he was sitting in the shop window.

'And he'll learn loads more! Anything you want to teach him!' the shopkeeper had said.

However, since the parrot had joined the Zep household, he had remained stubbornly silent.

'What's your name?' they asked him. Silence.

'Go on. Say hello to your new dad! Hello!' Grandpa begged. Nothing.

'But he *can* talk. I swear I heard him with my own ears,' Imelda protested.

'He's just being contrary,' Diomira finally concluded. Having learned from her experiences with stubborn children, she decided to give him an order that was the exact opposite of what she really wanted him to do.

She stood in front of him and, giving him a stern look, she said, 'Shut up!'

'Shut up!' the bird instantly responded.

'He can talk! He can talk!' the girls cheered,

glad they hadn't wasted all the money they'd patiently saved for their grandpa's present.

They'd got a bit too excited though. After that, no amount of flattery or threats could persuade the parrot to say a sentence, a word or a syllable other than 'Shut up!'.

I'm sure you'll agree that he doesn't really count as a talking parrot.

So 'Shut-up' became the bird's name. That was what they called him, and that was how he always responded, which soon put an end to any conversation.

Shut-up usually spent his time on his perch, munching away on sunflower seeds. He wasn't tied to the perch, but even though his long feathers had never been clipped, no one had ever seen him fly.

Ah, yes, let's get back to the parrot's bath time.

To carry out their plan, Emilia and Helena waited for an afternoon when their big sisters would be out.

Grandpa had gone for an afternoon nap in his room on the top floor and Diomira was dozing in the kitchen, her arms folded on the table and her forehead resting on her latest crossword magazine.

Sibylla was awake and gurgling at the flies buzzing above her crib, but the two conspirators didn't consider her a threat.

Ever so slowly, Emilia crept up behind Shut-up and grabbed him, holding his wings tightly with one hand and shutting his beak with the other, so that he wouldn't squawk.

Helena had already prepared Sibylla's bath tub, and was ready and waiting with soap and a towel.

In the blink of an eye, almost before he

realised what was going on, poor Shut-up found himself soaking wet.

The two girls, however, had imagined that once he was in the water he'd let them wash him, just as calmly as Sibylla. Instead though, the parrot managed to free his beak and wings and started to struggle furiously, splashing water, pecking blindly, and squawking with all the breath he had in his little lungs.

Then he slipped out of Emilia's hands and, dripping water and foam everywhere, he flew up on to the curtain rail, which was so high that no one would be able to catch him without a ladder.

The two girls started arguing:

'You were the one who scared him away!'

'You let go of his beak. And look what he did to me!'

'Serves you right. I'm not playing with you any more!'

But then a most extraordinary thing happened.

All the way up there, the drenched parrot was shivering with cold and squawking and grumbling away at the two girls when, suddenly, a soft and gentle cooing sound came from Sibylla's crib.

Shut-up opened his wings, puffed up his feathers and took off from the curtain rail, clearly speaking these words: 'Here I am, mistress!'

As if that weren't enough, as he flew over Emilia and Helena, who were looking up at him, all the water that had soaked his feathers formed a cloud and rained down on to the two girls, drenching them from head to toe.

Now perfectly dry, the parrot perched on the edge of the crib and repeated in an obedient voice, 'Here I am, mistress.'

'That's incredible!' Grandpa exclaimed later, when they told him what had happened. 'Someone must have taught him to say it before he came to live with us.'

Everyone was sure that he hadn't learned it from them. For one thing, it was Grandpa who was his owner now, so the parrot should have been saying 'master', not 'mistress'.

'So how come he's only remembered it now, after living with us for three years?' Wanda wondered.

'I'm sure I never heard him say that at the shop,' Imelda added.

'Do you think he'll say it again?' said Cassandra, and she decided to find out straightaway.

'Come on, Shut-up! Come to me!'

But Shut-up didn't move and he remained silent – and he didn't repeat the phrase to any other member of the family.

Diomira sighed. 'He's forgotten it again!' she said.

However, later that day, when Sibylla woke up and gave one of her usual gurgles, Shut-up darted from his perch like an arrow, squawking 'Here I am, mistress. I'm coming!' and he went to perch on the handle of her pushchair.

That, and the edge of Sibylla's crib, soon became his favourite perches, and whenever Grandpa or Diomira or one of the sisters took Sibylla out for a walk, the parrot refused to abandon his post. He went out with them, standing proud and straight on his perch and keeping a watchful eye on his little 'mistress'.

Mephisto the Cat

At this point, I should also mention Mephisto the cat.

You'll surely have wondered why, as Mephisto was available, Emilia and Helena had decided to give the parrot a bath instead of the cat, as any sensible child would have done. Well, the fact is that Mephisto was definitely NOT available. It's true that the cat lived in the same house as them, but he couldn't exactly be described as a tame pet.

Maybe he had been once, a long time ago,

when he'd first arrived as a birthday present for Imelda. Back then he'd been a timid little black kitten who took refuge in his mistress's arms at the slightest fright.

Imelda had been a big girl of seven at the time, but Cassandra was only four, and Helena had only just learned to walk. In spite of Imelda's protests, the two little girls subjected poor Mephisto to a long list of torments, including:

a. dragging him upstairs by the tail,
b. dressing him in doll's clothes,
c. combing his fur with their toy rake,
d. teaching him to 'dive' by throwing him into the garden pond,
e. and painting his claws with their mother's nail varnish.

Then Emilia came along and soon enough she learned to crawl on all fours. Her greatest pleasure was standing up – by grabbing Mephisto's whiskers and using them to pull herself upright with all her strength.

All of this happened when Imelda was at school and not around to defend her pet. So poor Mephisto had to learn to look after himself.

He did so with all the tools that nature had given him.

All it took to chase away his three tiny torturers was a few well-aimed scratches and some threatening hisses. However, by this point, Mephisto had become wary of every human being. He even started to avoid Imelda, maybe because he blamed her for abandoning him to her wicked little sisters.

Bit by bit, Mephisto became a wild cat. He was big, beautiful and glossy. He accepted the food that Diomira put out for him every day in a bowl on the kitchen steps. He always used the litterbox and, when he was sure he was alone in the house, he even allowed himself the luxury of sleeping on the sofa cushions.

However, he avoided all contact with the residents.

He preferred to hide up on top of a wardrobe, peering out over the edge to keep an eye on the comings and goings in the house.

It must be said, in Mephisto's favour, that he'd never tried to attack the parrot. Perhaps he felt some kind of sympathy for his fellow victim.

By the time of our story though, the littlest girls had completely forgotten that Mephisto had once been a tame and affectionate kitten, so it would never have occurred to them either to play with him kindly or to bother and torment him.

In fact, they were even a little afraid of him now. They were the ones who usually got out of the way when they saw that the big black cat was on the prowl.

Sibylla's Hair

Time passed. Sibylla was five months old now. Every week Wanda took a photo of her and sent it to their parents, so that they could see the little one's progress.

'What a darling!' their father exclaimed in the hotel room in the distant city where the tour had taken them. 'What a sweetheart! But why hasn't her hair started growing yet?'

'I've never seen such a smooth, pink, round little head,' said their mother, 'and I've had plenty of experience. After all, I've brought six other daughters into the world and watched them grow up!'

By now the tour was coming to an end. Just another few weeks and they would be back in their tatty old house, with the girls, Grandpa, Diomira, the cat and the parrot.

'Isn't that funny?' the girls' mother said, looking at the latest photo from Wanda. 'In the last four photographs, Sibylla's been wearing a bonnet.'

Their father pointed out that it wasn't always the same bonnet. One was white lace, one was light-blue knitted cotton, one was made of pink fabric with lime-green ribbons and the other was blue with yellow dots. They were four decidedly different designs.

'Maybe there's a heatwave,' their mother said, 'and they don't want her to get sunstroke when they take her out for a walk. It must be Diomira's doing.'

However, it was all down to Tabitha. She'd come up with the idea of using bonnets to hide a shocking fact from their parents: Sibylla's hair had finally started to grow.

But it wasn't brown like hers or blonde like Cassandra's. No. It was red.

Red as a flame, red as a beetroot, red as a ripe cherry, red as the inside of a watermelon. It was just a little sprinkling of hairs, here and there, soft as a duckling's feathers. But they were red – and no one in the family had ever had red hair.

Their poor mother had really been hoping to win the contest, with four blonde daughters to three brunettes! And their poor father had dreamed that the dark curls on Sibylla's head would make him the winner!

'It's pointless trying to keep it hidden,' Grandpa protested. 'Sooner or later they're going to find out. So we might as well tell them right away.'

As he was old and wise, his granddaughters eventually listened to his advice.

So when their father opened up the latest photograph in the lobby of the hotel in Vienna (it was just a week until their return), he found himself looking at a photograph of Sibylla with a bare head and a lock of flame-coloured hair tied up with a green ribbon.

We're also sending you some proof so that you don't think it's just a trick of the camera,

wrote Wanda.

I'm sorry. I know you'll be disappointed, but I hope you'll consider it a draw. I also want you to know that I can't face the thought of a baby number eight, probably yet another sister. If that happens, I'm afraid I'll have to consider running away from home and taking Diomira with me. And then who'll look after the little ones?

'She's right,' said their father. 'Seven's more than enough. You know, I think the colour of Sibylla's hair is a sign. And the sign says "STOP"!'

'So do I,' said their mother. 'I work, work, work, and I earn all this money . . . If we had only two children, we'd be filthy rich, with a swimming pool, a yacht, a chauffeur and a butler. Instead we just barely manage to pay Diomira's salary and to send all the girls to school dressed properly. An eighth child would definitely break the bank. Sibylla has to be the last one.'

'The last and the sweetest of all, with her

beautiful red hair,' their father concluded. 'Oh, I'm dying to give her a cuddle!'

'Me too,' said their mother. 'Being apart for five months was far too long. But now we're going to make up for lost time!'

Sibylla Learns to Walk

Their parents' visit lasted a couple of months this time, and Diomira went on holiday for a well-deserved rest. Zac also took some time off from the library to accompany his aunt to the mountains, and his stand-in was a rather drippy young woman who fluttered her eyelashes at everyone, even the revolting young man who was so fond of black magic.

Mrs Zep was an excellent actress, but a terrible housewife. Mr Zep wasn't much better and neither was Grandpa. So the six sisters looked after the house, including little Emilia and Helena, who were in charge of taking out the rubbish and watering the plants in the garden.

Grandpa took the breakfast tray to the girls' mother and father, who stayed in bed until late, being pampered and telling everyone about all the extraordinary things that had happened on their tour.

This time though, their daughters also had a few extraordinary things to tell them in return: Sibylla could float, Shut-up had spoken, and . . . none of the mirrors in the house reflected their baby sister.

It was Wanda who had discovered this strange fact. Ever since she'd fallen for a boy at school, a certain Sigfrido Garlasconi, who paid her absolutely no attention whatsoever, she'd been spending a lot of her time in front of the mirror.

She made up her eyes, experimented with contouring her cheeks to make her face look slimmer, constantly changed her hairstyle and pulled a thousand silly faces, while Tabitha and Cassandra hid behind the coat stand, giggling like crazy.

One Sunday morning, Wanda had put on some eyeshadow in a pretty shade of cyclamen, which Diomira said made her look like an angora rabbit. Wanda was convinced she looked amazing and, as she walked down the hallway to the garden, with Sibylla in her arms, she took one last look in the mirror to contemplate her reflection.

But she was stunned to see herself standing there all alone, with her arms wrapped around nothing. Sibylla was still there, with her little head resting on Wanda's shoulder, warm, heavy, solid . . . but the mirror showed no reflection of her.

'She really is a very special little girl!' Grandpa had said, and Sibylla's big sisters had agreed.

After all, what harm did it do? You don't need a reflection to be healthy!

'At least when she's your age, she won't be able to get up to the same silliness as you,' Diomira said to Wanda.

As her sisters told them this story, Sibylla was having fun on her parents' double bed, crawling around on all fours, climbing up her mum and dad as if they were mountains, and playing hide and seek under the covers with excited little squeaks.

'She'll be walking before too long,' sighed her mother, looking at her tenderly. 'It's such a shame that babies grow so fast!'

One morning, Sibylla was all alone on the bed.

Dad was in the bathroom, singing in the shower. Mum was leaning out of the window, chatting with Grandpa, who was down in the garden.

Wanda had just finished sweeping up the breakfast crumbs and was taking away the tray with the dirty cups and plates. The broom was leaning against the wall next to the bedside table.

Very quietly, holding on to the quilt, Sibylla slipped down from the bed. She crawled across the floor on all fours, took hold of the broom and . . .

'Mum! Sibylla's walking!' squealed Imelda, who had just entered the room, followed at a safe distance by Mephisto.

Her mother turned around and gasped.

Sibylla really was walking, holding on to the broom. But she wasn't just using it as a support. It was the broom itself that was moving – and taking Sibylla for a walk!

'Good heavens!' said her mother, collapsing into a chair, her face as white as a sheet.

'Ba-ba!' chuckled Sibylla, waving happily at

her mother with her free hand.

She went around the room three or four times, becoming more and more confident. Then she tilted the broom and climbed on to it like a horse, holding on firmly with both her hands.

The broom quivered and gently rose . . .

'Mum! Sibylla's flying!' exclaimed Helena.

'This really is too much!' sighed the girls'
mother. And she fainted.

Luckily she was already sitting down, so she
just slumped back in her chair and didn't even
get a bump or a bruise.

Don't go thinking that Sibylla flew to dizzying
heights though. She didn't touch the ceiling
or the light, for instance, or aim for the open
window. Wisely, the broom kept to within just a
few centimetres of the floor, hovering over a soft
rug.

However, even though it wasn't that high,
there could be no doubt about it: Sibylla was
flying on a broomstick.

As if that wasn't enough, when she finally
decided to land on the bed, with a lovely little
pirouette, Mephisto jumped up, walked over to
her and started purring and rubbing his head on
her back.

Yes, Mephisto, who hadn't allowed a human being to touch him or even get close to him for at least six years!

'That really is the limit!' groaned the girls' mother, who had come round by now, with the help of a few slaps from Imelda. 'Now all we need is for Mephisto to start saying "Here I am, mistress," too.'

The black cat gave her a look of disdain. *Stupid woman*! his sparkling eyes seemed to say. *Don't you know that cats can't talk?* But when Sibylla, squealing with joy, grabbed his tail and tried to pick him up, rather than struggling and flashing his claws, the cat just rubbed against her and purred twice as loud, with the most satisfied look in the world.

William Who?

It was time for the girls' parents to leave again. The director of an important theatre in London had invited them to take part in a Shakespeare festival, and their mother was going to perform in front of the Queen of England.

Diomira would be back from the mountains in only five days' time, but they couldn't put off their departure.

'Don't worry. I'm here,' said Grandpa. 'And the older girls are big enough now to help me look after their little sisters.'

'We're a bit worried about Sibylla,' sighed the girls' father. 'We've never seen a child behave this way before.'

'And we certainly should know a thing or two about children by now,' added their mother. 'But Sibylla is so unpredictable! Are you sure she's not too much for you to handle?'

'Calm down, Mum,' said Wanda reassuringly. 'What's there to worry about? Sibylla's fine. She's eating, sleeping and growing as she should, according to all the doctor's charts, and she's always in a good mood. And now she's walking by herself too. So why do you think something bad is going to happen?'

'That broom . . . She could fall off it and . . .'

'But you saw for yourself that she flies really low. And she holds on tight. Anyway, just to put your mind at ease, we'll keep all the brooms locked away in the cupboard, out of Sibylla's reach.'

Eventually, they managed to persuade their parents that it would be fine to leave Sibylla with them. Their mother was already rehearsing to herself, running over the lines of the part she'd be performing for the Queen.

The next day, Emilia and Helena started arguing again and tormenting the parrot and bothering Tabitha and Cassandra.

'Oh, when's Diomira getting back?' Tabitha wailed.

'Come on, let's go to the library,' her sister suggested. 'At least we'll have some peace there.'

Before leaving, their mother had promised that they could come over to England to watch some plays at the festival. Cassandra and Tabitha had decided to read some of Shakespeare's works first, so that they wouldn't make a fool of themselves.

So they went to the library and asked for something by Shakespeare. They didn't really mind what it was.

The young woman who was standing in for Zac was more interested in flirting with the male readers. Without even looking at the two girls, she muttered, 'William who? Shakespeare? Sounds vaguely familiar, but . . .'

She quickly scanned the letter S in the library catalogue and said, 'No. Sorry. We don't have anything by him. Is he a new author?'

'I'm talking about Shakespeare! S-H-A-K-E-S-P-E-A-R-E!' said Cassandra, spelling out the name. She'd read it so many times before in her mother's scripts and in the reviews of her plays that she could have spelled it backwards. Meanwhile, Tabitha leaned forward and pointed at an entry in the catalogue. 'Look! There! Shakespeare.'

'Oh, right! Of course! Well, why didn't you say so?' the stand-in replied, without batting an eyelid. 'Okay. *Macbeth*. The reference number is T.12/23. I'll go and fetch it for you.'

Tabitha smiled to herself and thought, *If only Zac could see this!*

Five minutes later, the stand-in returned empty-handed.

'I'm sorry. Someone's already reading *Macbeth*.' She nodded towards the young man who was interested in black magic.

He had a stack of six or seven big books on his table and they looked very old.

'Come on, let's go and sit by him,' Cassandra said to Tabitha. 'Maybe he's reading something else and we can borrow *Macbeth* for a bit, just to have a quick look. You know, we might not like it, and then there's no point waiting.'

So, overcoming their disgust for his greasy hair, his greenish teeth and his pimply cheeks, they approached him, and Tabitha politely asked the young man, speaking in a whisper, as you always should in a library: 'Excuse me, if you're not reading it right now, could we please take a look at Shakespeare's *Macbeth*?'

With a sigh and a tut, Alfonso Terribile – by this point I'm sure you've already recognised him, my dear readers – glanced up from his notes and said, 'That is indeed precisely what I'm reading right now. Would you please just shut up and wait your turn?'

The two sisters looked hopefully at the stack of books that their neighbour still had to consult. If he wanted to look at all of them this afternoon, he'd surely be finished with *Macbeth* before too long.

'Then I'll do my geography homework while I'm waiting. I have to hand it in on Friday,' said Tabitha, settling down at the table.

'And I'll finish that essay for English,' said Cassandra.

Cassandra was a champion at essay-writing. This time the title was: 'The Most Interesting Person in my Family'.

Normally she'd have thought it was a stupid title. All the older Zep sisters had already had to write a similar essay at school at some point. They'd chosen Grandpa, or Diomira, or Mum, and they'd just written the usual kind of things.

My grandfather's name is Lindoro. He was named after a character in an opera by Rossini, because his mother was a huge opera fan.

Or

My mum is an actress and she looks so beautiful when she dies on stage with all that fake blood on her satin dress and beautiful music that makes you cry.

And so on.

Of course, that was before Sibylla was born, with all her extraordinary abilities.

My sister, wrote Cassandra, *is really amazing*, and she went on to describe all the strange things about Sibylla, from the red hair that didn't fit in with the rest of the family, to the mirrors, the broom, and the parrot that obeyed her and called her mistress.

In the meantime, Tabitha was getting bored of looking through the atlas and noting down the names of rivers. She kept glancing across at Alfonso Terribile to see if he'd finished reading *Macbeth*.

Finally the young man put down the book and picked up another one, after scribbling something in his notebook.

Tabitha grabbed the Shakespeare, opened it at random and started reading: '*Fillet of a fenny snake, in the cauldron boil and bake, eye of newt and toe of frog, wool of bat and tongue of dog, adder's fork and blind-worm's sting, lizard's leg and owlet's wing. For a charm of powerful trouble, like a hell-broth boil and bubble.*'

Mmm, what a tasty recipe, Tabitha thought, in disgust. *That must be why he was reading the book! Maybe it's better if I start at the beginning . . .*

The play began with a big storm, thunder and lightning, three witches, a grey cat called Graymalkin and a toad called Paddock. The witches parted company and agreed to meet later. Then they disappeared, dissolving into the misty air.

After that, some kings and soldiers started saying things that were impossible to understand, at least for Tabitha, who was baffled by about half of the words on the page.

Maybe I should look them up in the dictionary, she thought, *but it's no fun reading a book that way.* Bored, she started fidgeting in her seat.

'Would you please stop wriggling around?' the young man said rudely, with a blast of his bad breath.

'That's it. I'm off!' said Tabitha, stepping back to avoid the smell. 'Come on,

Cassandra, you too. You can finish your essay at home!'

'It's already done,' replied Cassandra, slipping off her chair and waving the neat copy of her essay in the air to dry the ink.

She didn't notice that she'd left the rough draft on the table. But Alfonso did.

'What a couple of little louts!' he said loudly. 'Brats of that age shouldn't be allowed in the reading room. Look,' he said to the stand-in librarian, 'they've left their rubbish on the table!'

'Oh, really? Goodness, you're right. Thanks for pointing it out!' she replied, with a flirtatious smile.

Alfonso buried his nose in his stained and crumpled notebook and continued writing, furiously underlining some of the words.

His notes read:

How to identify a witch:

1. She has red hair.
2. Mirrors don't show her reflection.
3. If she's thrown into water with her hands and feet tied, she'll float instead of sinking.
4. She is usually accompanied by her familiars, magical animals like black cats or owls, which talk to her and obey her every command.
5. She flies on her broomstick to meet others of her kind at their witches' sabbath, on nights with a full moon.
6. She is one in a line of seven sisters that was not interrupted by the birth of any males.

How to make a witch do whatever you tell her

Once you're certain that you've found a witch, every means of capturing her is allowed, including cunning, violence and lies.

When you've caught her, lock her up in a damp, dark place. Leave her without food for two weeks. Then whip her thirteen times on the little toes with willow branches soaked in seawater. Scorch her big toes with a candle flame and threaten to burn her at the stake. By this point, in order to be released, she'll agree to do whatever you say.

He had placed a large question mark beside point number six because, unfortunately, the information was incomplete. Alfonso had obtained the fact from an ancient volume whose pages were not only musty and faded, but had also been nibbled here and there by a mouse. As a result, some of the sentences were impossible to understand, and Alfonso hadn't managed to work out if the rule was complete or if some important details were missing.

Alfonso Sniffs Out a Witch

Finishing his notes with a flourish, Alfonso Terribile slammed shut the last book of magic, raising a cloud of ancient dust above the library table. Then he started scratching his head frantically, sprinkling the books with a shower of dandruff.

He was both furious and desperate.

What was the point of knowing all about witches and their habits if you had no idea where to meet one in the flesh?

The deadline in Great-Uncle Sempronio's

will was getting closer and closer. He had only a month left now – thirty miserable days – to find a witch, to woo her (that's if she was single, of course) and to convince her to marry him. If he didn't, it was goodbye to Great-Uncle Sempronio's fortune for ever.

Don't imagine that Alfonso had just been twiddling his thumbs in the meantime though.

Quite the contrary, in fact. He'd advertised in newspapers, hired private investigators, and had himself visited all the places he could imagine that a witch might go.

But it had all been in vain.

So you can imagine just how irritable he was feeling that day, as he sat there with his pencil, popping the pimples on his chin.

But then, just as he reached his moment of deepest despair, his gaze fell on the rough draft of Cassandra's essay, and he automatically read the first lines.

Zac's stand-in heard a muffled yell and saw Black Magic Boy (everyone in the library knew him by that name) wildly underlining sentences with a red pen.

Alfonso couldn't believe his eyes. *There's no doubt about it*, he thought. *This has to be a witch . . . And she must be a young witch, if she's that brat's sister. And it doesn't say that she's already married!*

Unfortunately it didn't say that she was a one-year-old baby either, but that thought didn't even occur to poor Alfonso.

Even though he'd found himself in the middle of such an extraordinary adventure, he was still a remarkably unimaginative young man, and he simply wasn't capable of realising that if witches existed, then they must be all kinds of different ages, just like everyone else. He had been told to marry one, and so he imagined that somehow all witches must be able to get married.

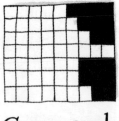

Crosswords

I realise, my dear readers, that by this point you will be wondering: *Why did none of the Zep family have any suspicions about Sibylla? Why did none of her strange powers – particularly her ability to fly on a broomstick – never make anyone think that the little girl might be a witch?*

That's a very good point. But the truth is that the Zeps were modern, educated people. They were used to taking a scientific approach to the world around them. They despised superstition and had never been interested in fairy tales and legends, and so they knew absolutely nothing about the various ways to recognise a witch. They had much better things to do than pore over old books of magic!

The only one with the slightest suspicion was Diomira. This wasn't because of Sibylla's strange behaviour, however, which didn't surprise her at all – as an expert nanny, she knew every baby was different and that you have to accept everyone as they are. No, her suspicions had been roused during her recent holiday – and it was all because of a crossword.

Diomira was a very creative woman and she was not content just to solve the crosswords she found ready and waiting in the newspaper.

Every now and then she also took part in competitions, submitting super-complicated crosswords that she made up herself.

One afternoon, while she was sunbathing in a deckchair beside a glacier, she had decided to try making a crossword puzzle using the names of her 'little girls', as she insisted on calling all the Zep sisters.

And she had started by writing them down horizontally.

Then she had checked the vertical columns. (Go on, take a look for yourself). And she had gasped.

'What's wrong, Auntie?' asked Zac, who was sunbathing beside her and sipping a glass of minty milk.

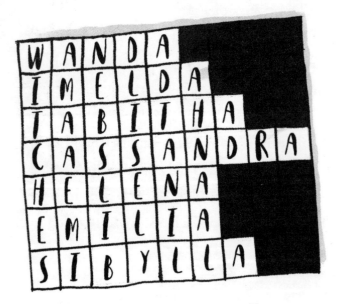

She wrote a word at the top of the paper. 'Look what my little girls' initials spell out when you arrange them in order of age . . . *WITCHES*! I wonder if their parents did it on purpose? Or if they even realised when they chose their names . . .'

'I wouldn't have thought so,' said Zac slowly. 'That doesn't seem like them. And if they'd noticed, they're such chatterboxes that they'd have had to mention it. It must just be a coincidence.'

'But it still seems strange. Could it mean something? I don't know, some kind of hidden significance . . .'

'Don't be daft, Auntie. Stop talking nonsense!' Zac had exclaimed, crumpling the sheet of paper into a ball and putting it in his pocket. 'Go and sit in the shade! The sun's clearly gone to your head, or you wouldn't be coming out with such silliness!'

Diomira burst out laughing and, before long, she'd forgotten all about the whole business.

Some days later – it was the morning of the day when Alfonso made his big discovery – she returned home.

By then, she had completely forgotten about the crossword puzzle, as she was just about the angriest she had ever been.

As was usual after she'd been away, the house was dirty and untidy. The sink was full of dishes to wash, the garden choked with weeds, the girls' clothes torn and stained, the fridge empty and some of the goldfish in the pond had died of indigestion.

She'd been expecting that though. She'd always known the Zep family weren't very good at housework.

What she hadn't expected was the sight of her

two little darlings, Tabitha and Cassandra, who welcomed her with heads shaved as smooth as billiard balls.

Wanda, on the other hand, had flame-red hair, even brighter than Sibylla's.

'What on earth has happened to you?' asked Diomira with her hands on her hips.

'Imelda's chemistry experiment,' answered Cassandra.

As soon as their parents had left, Imelda, who was the most scientifically minded of the sisters, had invented a hair dye based on some of the herbs from the garden combined with a bunch of chemicals.

She wanted to experiment on the entire family, but Grandpa had fiercely defended his few remaining hairs and had forbidden her to dye the youngest sisters' hair.

'The rest of you are old enough to decide for yourselves. But I hope you've got more sense!'

However, the girls turned out not to have much sense at all, because all three of them meekly submitted to Imelda's dye, and as a result Wanda's hair turned red, which wasn't too bad, but Cassandra's went as green as a pea and Tabitha's was deep purple.

'Don't worry. It's only temporary,' Imelda said, trying to calm them down.

The two girls were so embarrassed walking around with strangely coloured hair that they decided they had no alternative but to shave it all off.

'Oh, really?' said Diomira. 'And what did they say at school?'

'We're not going to school. Grandpa says he'll write us a note to say we're staying at home "for family reasons". They'll tell us what our homework is, and we'll do it all at home.'

'You pair of little idiots! You deserve a good hiding!'

'They've already been punished enough,' said Grandpa. 'Imagine having to spend all day bored at home for a fortnight! No friends, no cinema, no bikes, no swimming pool, no library!'

'Okay, okay!' muttered Diomira, calming down. 'Well, let's hope at least it'll teach you a lesson!'

A Romantic Drama
in the Library

Let's get back to Alfonso though, in the library, where he's been hit by a worrying doubt.

That essay . . . Is it true or is it just a story? he wondered. *Does this red-headed sister who flies on a broomstick really exist, or did the little brat make it all up to impress her teacher?*

He had to find out – and soon!

Those two little horrors seem to be regular visitors to the library, he thought. *I bet the librarian will know who they are – and all about the rest of the family too.*

Zac's stand-in watched nervously as the man of her dreams stood up and approached her desk with a secretive air about him.

Ooh, how exciting! she squealed inwardly. *He's going to ask me out on a date!*

So I'm sure you can imagine how upset she was when he asked her if she happened to know if the two girls who had just left had an older sister.

It just so happened that she did indeed know the Zep family, at least by sight.

'They certainly do,' she replied sourly. 'In fact, they have two, each more unpleasant than the other.' (That was just jealousy though, because she didn't really know them at all.)

'And what are they like? I mean, what colour is their hair?' the young man persisted.

'One's dark-haired, as black as a crow. Oh, and ugly, so ugly . . .' began the disappointed stand-in, referring to Imelda.

'And the other?' Alfonso asked impatiently.

If I tell him the oldest one is a blonde, he'll imagine – I don't know – some beautiful woman like the singers and dancers on TV, thought the jealous stand-in, so she said in a hesitant voice: 'Oh, I don't know . . . It's fair, kind of mousy, I guess. But, hey, I wouldn't advise asking that one out. She's a real witch!'

She gave a satisfied sigh, sure that she'd eliminated a rival.

Alfonso, however, was over the moon. He could already feel the weight of Great-Uncle Sempronio's fifty million in his pockets, and it was a very pleasant weight, a weight that, rather than dragging him down, made him float up into the air like a big red balloon.

'Could you tell me their names? And their address?' he demanded, not even noticing that the jealous librarian was about to burst into tears.

'No idea,' she spat.

'But if those brats – I mean, those two little girls – are members of the library, then their details will be in your membership book,' Alfonso insisted. He was so close to his goal and he didn't intend to give up easily.

The stand-in began to cry with anger. 'That's enough. Please leave now!'

Two or three old people who were reading newspapers lifted their heads and looked at them disapprovingly. And who knows what would have happened next if Zac had not chosen that very moment to return to work, beautifully tanned and rested after his holiday with Aunt Diomira?

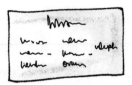

Seven Witches

Zac was a bright young man and he immediately took charge.

He comforted the stand-in librarian and sent her to splash cold water on her face.

He listened politely to Alfonso's request, and then answered very firmly that such information was private.

Struggling to contain his disappointment, Alfonso Terribile decided to wait until the following day. He certainly didn't intend to speak to the two brats, but would follow them when they went home, to find out where they lived.

However, the two brats didn't show up in the reading room, and they didn't set foot in the library for the rest of the week either.

Zac was also puzzled by their absence, because Diomira hadn't told him about Imelda's chemistry experiment and its disastrous consequences.

But while Zac was puzzled, Alfonso Terribile was furious. There was an eligible young witch somewhere nearby – and he had no idea how to get his hands on her!

All the while, his precious time was trickling away.

On the seventh day, however, his luck appeared to change. Zac had popped out for a moment to go to the loo, leaving a big book open on the counter. Alfonso crept closer.

I bet the brats' address is in that book, he

thought. But all it contained was a list of books with their prices and the date they'd been added to the collection.

However, a sheet of paper had fallen from Zac's pocket and was now lying on the floor. Without seeing it, Alfonso stepped on the paper, slipped on it, glared down, and then jumped.

At the top of the paper, he could see the word *WITCHES* and, beneath it, a list of names.

Blissfully happy, unable to believe his good luck, Alfonso Terribile picked up the paper and dashed back to his table to read it in peace.

Good heavens! That lying librarian not only knew the two brats' witchy sister, but he actually appeared to know others of her kind. There were their names, listed on the piece of paper. According to the books Alfonso had been consulting in the previous months, they were real witches' names too. Like Iheliim and Banenli, and so on.

I'm sure I don't need to point out that we've already encountered this piece of paper, by the way, but to refresh your memories, take a look at page 78.

Hallelujah, thought Alfonso. *Now I just need to make the birdie sing.* (The birdie was, of course, Zac). The best plan, he decided, was to act like he didn't really care.

'Oh you dropped this, and I accidentally stepped on it,' he said when Zac returned to the reading room. 'I hope it's not important.'

'Oh, no, it's nothing!' Zac replied with a smile. 'Just one of my aunt's scribbles. She likes playing around with words. They're the names of her girls . . . Oh, that reminds me! Excuse me, I need to make a phone call.'

Alfonso's brain started whirring away at a phenomenal speed.

'*Her girls*'? he thought. *So this aunt must know them well. Maybe she's related to them too. One*

*of the seven has to be the brats' witchy sister. Yes,
I noticed that they seemed quite friendly with the
librarian . . . Life is so unfair! I'm about to lose
fifty million because I can't find a single witch –
and he knows at least seven of them!*

Zac had meanwhile dialled a telephone
number and was saying: 'Hello? Is that the
Zeps? Is that you, Auntie? Is everything okay
over there? Has everyone got flu or something? I
was just wondering why Tabitha and Cassandra
haven't been around all week.'

The Girl With the Red Hair

Alfonso Terribile didn't stay around to listen to the rest of the conversation, but rushed off to look up the name Zep. He could find only one Zep family in the telephone directory but, luckily, they lived about a hundred metres from the library, in Via Giovanna d'Arco, at number thirteen.

Without wasting any time, Alfonso hurried out of the library and headed to that address. Finding the gate open, he went into the garden and hid behind a bush to wait, his heart pounding like crazy.

Calm down, Alfonso! Calm down! he told himself. *Remember that you still have to convince the girl to marry you. You need to make a good impression on her. You've got to win her over. To woo her and wed her.* He'd decided that he would resort to kidnapping and imprisonment only if the situation became desperate. This wasn't out of kindness, of course, but because he didn't have a suitable space for locking up a wilful witch and whipping her little toes with willow branches and all the rest.

That's awful, right? If Alfonso hadn't been such an ignorant fool, he'd have realised that those lines, copied from a mouldy book that was centuries old, were not only a legend but had also been invented at a time when men were even more wild and primitive than they are now. Whipping someone's little toes is a very uncomfortable operation too, as you have to lie down on your tummy on the floor, and it's not very easy to take good aim.

Anyway, as he needed to marry her, it would be better if his future wife agreed to the plan of her own free will. Otherwise, even with his fifty million, she could make his married life a misery. Even an idiot like Alfonso could work that out.

But if she doesn't appreciate my charms, then I won't hesitate to resort to stronger measures! he thought, as he chewed on the filter of his tenth cigarette.

It was a bright afternoon in March. Leaning against the wall of the house, there were seven ladies' bicycles, in a range of sizes.

Aha, the witch is indeed one in a line of seven sisters! Alfonso Terribile thought in delight, unaware that the two largest bicycles belonged to the girls' mother and Diomira, and Sibylla was too young for a bike, of course.

Then, on the washing line, he spotted seven

pleated tartan skirts, also in various sizes.

I've done it! I've found her! he silently rejoiced.
What he didn't know was that all of the kilts
belonged to Grandpa. As a young man, Grandpa
had performed for a number of seasons as an
extra in *Lucia di Lammermoor*, an opera set
in Scotland, and he'd kept his costumes as a
precious heirloom for the family. And that was
the day Diomira had chosen to air them to get
rid of the smell of mothballs.

Up against the gate, there was an old-fashioned
broom: a bundle of twigs tied to a gnarled and
sturdy handle.

Finally! My work is done! thought Alfonso,
expecting the girl of his dreams to appear at any
moment, to leap on to her magic steed and to fly
with him straight to the altar.

He didn't care what kind of person she was:
stupid or intelligent, kind or cruel. All that
mattered to him was the fifty million.

He didn't even try to imagine what the young witch might look like. He knew he would be able to recognise her by the colour of her hair, and that was enough.

He waited and waited. The first to leave the house was Imelda. She was carrying two large empty bags and a piece of paper: the shopping list, which she gave one last look before jumping on to her bike and riding off towards the supermarket, pedalling away with her wavy black hair blowing in the breeze.

Black hair . . . so it can't be her . . . thought Alfonso, tossing the butt of his fifteenth cigarette on the ground.

Then Helena appeared. She came to the door and put a bowl of milk on the steps, for the cat.

Number two! But this one has black hair too and she's definitely too young . . . pondered Alfonso.

Even more disappointing, in terms of both

age and hair colour, was the appearance of Emilia on the first-floor balcony, who'd come out to throw crumbs for the goldfish in the garden pond.

And three! thought Alfonso, patiently waiting for the other four sisters to emerge.

But then the garage door swung open and two BOYS came out, carrying spanners and a bicycle pump. They were wearing oil-stained blue overalls and had very short hair indeed – they were practically skinheads!

Two boys! Alfonso wailed inwardly. *But the witch has to be part of an uninterrupted line of seven sisters!*

His knees felt weak with disappointment, and a slight dizziness made him sway, as the two boys walked by without noticing him hidden among the leaves and branches. Alfonso could see them though, and they passed within a hand's breadth of his face. He jumped as he recognised the faces and voices of the two brats from the library.

Why on earth had they disguised themselves like that? They'd almost scared the life out of him.

But their presence in the garden was the confirmation, if he'd needed it, that he was on the right track with the Zeps.

Alfonso felt like a new man.

'And five!' he sighed with relief, spitting the butt of his thirtieth cigarette on to the ground.

But then the broom flashed by, right under his nose.

'Excuse me! What on earth do you think you're doing?!' Diomira growled at him. 'Go and drop cigarette butts in your own bushes, you filthy pig! And why are you in our garden anyway? Clear off! Go on! Scram! Away with you!'

And six! he thought, as Diomira swept him back out through the garden gate. Then he realised, *Ah, but she can't be the sixth sister. She's too old. And she has grey hair, not red. But she was pretty quick with that broom, which is very suspicious . . . and as for the hair, the people in this house have a dangerous fondness for disguises.*

So, rather than walking away, he grabbed Diomira's hair and gave it a tug, just to make sure it wasn't a wig.

'Get your hands off me, you hoodlum!' shrieked Diomira, slapping him across the face.

'Owww!' wailed Alfonso, opening his mouth wide.

'And try brushing your teeth occasionally!' the housekeeper added furiously, slamming the gate and firmly bolting it.

Alfonso crouched down behind a lamp post. 'The things I have to put up with for this miserable fifty million!' he whined to himself.

But he was more determined than ever to wait for the last two sisters to appear. One of them had to be the witch of his dreams.

After a while, the gate squeaked and Grandpa brought out a bag of rubbish.

He doesn't count, thought Alfonso, who was starting to get really irritable now.

At the end of the road, a bicycle bell rang out, DRIING DRIIINNG, and around the corner came a beautiful girl who was pedalling energetically and carrying two heavy bags of food on the handlebars. She was wearing a blue woollen hat with a matching scarf fluttering behind her.

Ah, now she'd make a nice girlfriend, thought Alfonso. *It's a shame she's nothing to do with the Zeps.*

He'd seen Imelda, who was clearly going to the supermarket, and assumed that she was the only shopper in the family. It didn't occur to him that such a large family would need more groceries than one girl could transport on a bike.

So it came as a surprise when the girl in the blue hat braked as she arrived at the gate of number thirteen and hopped off her saddle to pull back the bolt.

She went into the garden, pushing her bike with one hand, and when she reached the door she took off her hat with the other hand, shaking on to her shoulders a mane of red wavy hair that gleamed like an autumn fire.

Stunned by this turn of events, Alfonso Terribile tripped over his own feet and crashed to the ground, hitting his head on the lamp post and giving himself a massive bump.

'Are you still here?' barked Diomira, hurrying outside and lifting him up by the collar of his jacket. She gave him a good shake and pushed him down the street, with a kick in the behind to help him on his way.

Alfonso Terribile staggered off, with the sky spinning crazily around his head and millions of birds twittering away. The stars were exploding like fireworks, even though it was only five in the afternoon.

Something extraordinary had happened: not only had he finally found the witch who would solve all his problems . . .

No! Better than that! he thought joyfully, even

though that alone would have made him wild with delight.

No, for the first time in his sad little life, Alfonso Terribile had fallen in love. And he had fallen in love with Wanda, the red-headed girl who would bring him all of Great-Uncle Sempronio's longed-for millions.

Talk about good luck!

At this point, I should perhaps explain that Alfonso's greed had caused him to lose all reason. While he had previously been just a poor idiot, now he had gone completely insane. If it had meant he would get his hands on the inheritance, he would happily have fallen in love with a giant tortoise, or maybe even a tree or a microwave oven.

All that time, Sibylla had been crawling about in her playpen by the apple tree, right under Alfonso's nose, reaching her arm through the bars in an attempt to grab the broom. She was wearing a green playsuit and a matching bonnet, which hid her hair.

Shut-up was perched silently on the playpen, and Mephisto, sitting behind the bars, had been staring suspiciously at the stranger, who hadn't paid any attention to the trio.

Poor Alfonso! That night he didn't sleep a wink, imagining that his misery would soon be over.

However, because that mouse had nibbled the manuscript, the careless young man was unaware of one crucial detail: to be a witch, she had to be not only one in a line of seven sisters, but also the LAST in the line . . .

A Persistent Suitor

The next morning, Alfonso Terribile decided to spruce himself up and go out to win the girl of his dreams.

By this point, convincing her to marry him was not enough. He was sure he could manage that in a jiffy, just by waving the fifty million under her nose.

No. Now the ambitious young man also wanted to be loved. (Just imagine how funny it would have been if he really had fallen in love with a microwave oven instead of a girl!)

So he put on his best suit, slicked down his hair with an entire tub of gel and, for the first time in about three years, he gave his teeth a quick brush. Then he went out in search of a flower shop and, after spending a long time haggling for a discount, he bought a large bouquet of red roses. He slipped one into his buttonhole and, all dressed up, he returned to his position in Via Giovanna d'Arco, outside number thirteen.

The girls were all at school, except for Cassandra and Tabitha, who were out in the garden, with woollen hats on their shaved heads, watering the daffodils around the pond.

Sibylla was outside too, in her playpen, all bundled up in a red playsuit, enjoying the spring sunshine.

As usual, the cat and the parrot were keeping her company.

And, also as usual, Alfonso Terribile, even

though they were right under his nose all morning, didn't think the trio worthy of any attention.

At around one o'clock, the young man finally heard voices and laughter at the end of the street and he saw Imelda coming. She rushed into the house, followed at some distance by Wanda, who was holding the two little ones by the hand, one on each side.

Alfonso would rather have talked to her in private, but he had little time to spare and he couldn't afford to miss this opportunity.

So he jumped out of his hiding place, stood in her way and, holding out the bouquet of roses with a deep bow, he declared: 'Miss Zep, please accept this tribute, which is not worthy of your beauty! Along with these roses, I lay my heart at your feet.'

Fascinated, Emilia and Helena looked down at the ground in front of Wanda's feet, but they didn't see a heart there.

'Liar!' said Emilia.

'I think he must be a loony,' whispered Helena.

'Excuse me?' said Wanda. 'I don't think I quite understand. What did you say?'

'Miss Zep,' replied Alfonso breathlessly. 'You are the most beautiful girl I've ever seen. I have been madly in love with you since the first moment I saw you. Will you marry me?'

'But I don't even know you . . .' Wanda protested.

'You're right. Let me introduce myself. I'm Alfonso Terribile. The sole heir of the late Sempronio Terribile, multi-millionaire. Marry me, and you'll be a multi-millionaire too.'

'But I'm only fifteen!' said Wanda. 'I still have to finish school. Then I want to go to university to study xenoarchaeology and . . .'

She didn't point out that she wasn't legally allowed to get married at her age anyway. The problem wasn't the law. It was that the man was really disgusting.

'Nonsense!' exclaimed Alfonso. 'Beautiful girls don't need to waste their time studying! They should focus on getting married as soon as they can. If possible, to a very rich young man. Like me.'

Wanda blasted him with a look of disapproval and, without answering, she went through the garden gate, dragging her sisters behind her.

'Wait!' cried Alfonso. 'Don't be like that! At least tell me your name! Is it Banenli maybe? Or Ltaorga? Or Aaraa?'

But Wanda had already gone inside and firmly closed the door behind her.

'Wanda's got a new boyfriend,' announced
Emilia to the rest of the family later, when they
were all sitting together at the dinner table.

'Why didn't you tell him that you're in love
with Sigfrido Garlasconi?' asked Imelda.

'Because it's none of his business. And it's
none of yours either.'

'Girls, girls! Be nice!' said Diomira, as she
dished up the soup. Deep down, she'd always
hoped that, once she'd finished her studies,
Wanda would marry her nephew Zac.

That evening and the whole night long, a strange
and mournful cry rang out beneath the windows
of the house on Via Giovanna d'Arco.

'Banenli! Ltaorga! Ibaoedl! Aaraaaaaa!'

Wanda was fast asleep, but Diomira kept

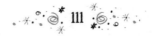

worrying and tossing and turning all night, not just because of the noise, which was keeping her awake, but also because of a nagging thought that was buzzing around inside her head like a particularly annoying mosquito: *I think I've heard those words somewhere before.* But she couldn't remember where or when, and she didn't like that at all. *Am I going senile?* she thought. *Before I know it, I won't be able to do my crossword puzzles any more.*

'Iheliim! Litnvei! Aaraaa!' shouted the stranger.

Grandpa climbed out of bed, with bare feet and in his pyjamas, and went to look out of the window. But it was a dark night and he didn't make a connection between the stranger who had been caught spying in the garden and the shadow wailing beneath the lamp post, waving a bunch of wilting roses.

He went back to bed and spent the rest of the

night awake, cursing the man who wouldn't let him sleep in peace.

Alfonso Does Not Quit

At lunchtime the next day, Wanda received a huge bouquet of yellow tulips and a box containing a diamond ring.

Every woman responds to the charm of jewellery, Alfonso had thought. *The size of the stone will show her just how much I love her — and how rich I am.*

As he still hadn't managed to find out the name of his beauty, he had addressed his gift to 'the magnificent girl with the flame-coloured hair who so kindly received my declaration of love yesterday'.

'Kindly?!' exclaimed Wanda indignantly. 'I didn't accept his flowers and I slammed the door in his face!'

'What are you going to do with the ring?' asked Tabitha curiously.

'You have to give it back to him!' Diomira said firmly.

'And how am I supposed to do that if I don't remember his name or know where he lives?' protested Wanda.

'Don't worry. He'll be back,' said Grandpa.

And indeed, the next day, Alfonso Terribile was waiting for Wanda at the school gates.

'You!' said Wanda as soon as she spotted him. And without giving him time to open his mouth, she fumbled around in her bag, took out the ring and deposited it in his hand.

'I don't like jewellery!' she said sharply. 'And I don't like creepy men!'

'But I love you!' protested Alfonso.

'I'm sorry,' replied Wanda. 'I don't love you. Please leave me alone.'

'But I can't live without you! I absolutely have to marry you. And soon! There's no time to lose.'

Wanda burst out laughing.

'Don't be silly. Can't you see that I'm just a schoolgirl? Go and find another girlfriend and stop getting under my feet.'

Angry and disappointed, Alfonso tried to protest, but Wanda joined a group of her friends and walked off, leaving him looking a little bit foolish.

Alfonso Resorts to Foul Means

Furious, Alfonso decided to change his plans. He didn't have time to waste wooing that flirt! There were only eighteen days left now until his deadline.

'As I can't win her by fair means, I shall have to resort to foul means instead. And it will be her fault entirely. After all, I started out with the very best of intentions.'

What he needed was a basement where he could lock up the witch.

Then he remembered that, in the library

courtyard, there were some windows at ground level, protected by bars.

He discovered that they were part of a large basement, packed with old books that were waiting to be restored. By flattering the former stand-in from the reading room, who was now substituting for the older lady on the lending desk, Alfonso Terribile managed to get close enough to steal the keys to the basement. He also located a container of seawater and a large bundle of fresh willow branches.

'And now it's just you and me, you ugly fool of a witch!' he said, rubbing his hands.

The Saturday after these events, Diomira awoke with a really bad backache.

'This blasted sciatica!' she said, crying with pain. 'I can't even get out of bed. And I really need to take Sibylla to the doctor's today for her check-up.'

'Don't worry,' said Wanda. 'I'll take her. You stay nice and warm in bed and concentrate on getting better.'

So Wanda gave Sibylla a good wash, brushed her hair, dressed her and put her in her pushchair. The cat and the parrot were ready and waiting by the front door.

'Oh, no!' said Wanda. 'The two of you aren't coming. We can get away with it when we go to the park, even if people laugh behind our backs when they see our little procession. But that poor doctor's already seen enough oddness, what with Sibylla floating and so on . . . Do you want him to think that our family's some kind of circus?'

'Come on, the two of you, into the kitchen,' said Grandpa. 'And don't pull those sad faces. We're not stealing your Sibylla. She'll be back home in an hour or so.'

Complaining pitifully, the creatures allowed themselves to be carried away into the kitchen, as Wanda left the house and pushed the pushchair towards the gate. Unaware of the danger, she quickly walked past the library and headed for the shortcut through the park.

At that time in the morning, no one else was around, so when Alfonso Terribile emerged from behind a bush, holding the kind of net that they use at the circus for wild animals, Wanda cried out 'Help! Heeeelp!' but it was no good.

No one heard her and no one saw the revolting young man creeping up on her.

Instinctively, Wanda leaned forward to pick up Sibylla from her pushchair and hugged her in her arms, so that when the net fell, it captured both of them, much to the annoyance of Alfonso Terribile, who only wanted to kidnap the big sister and would have been quite happy to abandon the little one in the park. He certainly didn't have time now to untangle the baby from the net.

'Well, you asked for it, you fool!' he said. 'Now the brat will have to come with you into the cosy little nest I've prepared!'

The basement was dark and filled with cobwebs. The books, piled up in stacks that reached the ceiling, smelled of mould. The rapid rustling in the darkest corner could only be mice.

Alfonso Terribile had nailed boards across the windows so that no one outside could see or hear what was happening down below.

Feeling safe now, Alfonso freed Sibylla from the net and placed her inside a box that had once contained an encyclopedia.

'You stay there and don't so much as breathe!' he said rudely.

'Ba-ba!' replied Sibylla.

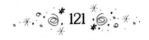

'Be quiet if you know what's good for you!'

'If you hurt my sister, I'll smash your face in!' said Wanda, struggling to escape.

Alfonso cackled. 'You just try it!' he said, picking up a thick rope, which he then looped through the net and used to tie Wanda to a pipe in the wall. 'For the last time, will you marry me? Yes or no?' he growled.

'Never!' replied Wanda, tugging really hard to free herself.

The rusty pipe snapped in two and a powerful jet of water soaked the prisoner, who went tumbling on to the floor!

Up on the second floor of the library, in the staff toilets, Zac froze, with his soapy hands in mid-air.

'Oh, why did the taps have to stop working right now?' he muttered. 'I'll have to call the caretaker to take a look at the plumbing.'

Back in the basement, Sibylla had managed to climb over the edge of the box and was venturing out among the piles of precariously balanced books.

Alfonso Terribile had picked Wanda up off the floor, but she was drenched from head to toe.

'And this is just the beginning!' he said. 'Prepare yourself for two weeks of complete fasting. Then we'll move on to the whipping.'

'Two weeks! No way!' replied Wanda. 'They'll be here to rescue us by tomorrow morning. Aaaa-chooo!'

Alfonso Terribile glared at her. That sneeze sounded like the start of a serious cold. Was the stupid girl ill now? That was all he needed! He hadn't thought to prepare for something like this! How could he take care of her and make sure she didn't die before the wedding? And what if she coughed all night and made the security guard suspicious?

It would be better to take immediate action.

He removed his shirt, which, for once, was perfectly clean, and held it out to Wanda.

'Dry yourself!' he ordered, untying her hands.

Wanda briskly rubbed her head, and . . . Alfonso Terribile let out a howl, staring at her with his eyes bulging out of their sockets.

The fact was that Wanda's home dye had faded a little with every shampooing, and thanks to her surprise soaking, the rest of the fiery redness had rubbed off on to Alfonso's shirt.

Her hair, now soaked and twisting like little snakes, had returned to its natural colour: as blonde as wheat.

'Betrayal! I've been deceived!' Alfonso yelled.

'You liar! Oh, I'm going to make you pay for this!'

But he didn't have time to do anything, because an object, hurled with force, slammed into his back and he fell flat on his face.

'Sibylla! Be careful! You could fall! Come down this instant!' Wanda shouted.

But Sibylla, as happy as could be, was flying around on an old broom that she'd found covered in cobwebs in a corner of the basement. She darted from one wall to the other just below the vaulted ceiling, then swooped down on Alfonso Terribile, whacking him with the broomstick.

Laughing as she soared back up to the ceiling, she pirouetted, and reared up in the air, as if to say: 'Look at me! Look how good I am!' But of course all that came out was 'Ba-ba-BAAA!'

In all the fun of the flying, her blue bonnet fell

off her head and Alfonso Terribile was startled to see her red curls.

He soon realised that he'd made a huge mistake, as it dawned upon him that the sentence the mouse had nibbled referred to the fact that the witch was always the LAST of seven sisters.

He cursed himself for being such an idiot and not working it out before. In a fraction of a second, he pulled himself together.

After all, there was nothing to worry about, was there? Even though it was unintentional, he'd still captured a young unmarried witch, and now he had her at his mercy.

He could subject HER to fasting and whipping, he could bend her to his will, he could marry her. He still had plenty of time.

This furious madman was not at all bothered that his future wife was still just a baby. All that mattered to him now was the inheritance.

Witch Hunt

Meanwhile, back at home, Diomira was still lying in her sickbed, all wrapped up under the covers, with six hot-water bottles and a shawl around her hips.

'If only I could just manage to take a little nap!' she fumed. 'If those two blasted beasts don't stop making such a racket, I swear I'll go downstairs and throttle them!'

Down in the kitchen, the cat and the parrot had been making an infernal din for about an hour now. Mephisto was scratching away at the

door and meowing mournfully. Shut-up kept
flapping his wings, shaking the handle
of the window with his beak, and sighing . . .

Then he started headbutting the glass and
screeching hysterically: 'Help! Help! Danger!
There's no time to lose! Alarm! Help!'

'Will you stop that at once!' Grandpa yelled,
throwing a wet dishcloth at Shut-up.

He didn't understand why the two creatures were
so upset. As far as he could see, there was nothing
to worry about. It was a morning like any other.
Most of the girls were at their dance classes. Wanda
and Sibylla had gone out just an hour ago and
should be back by lunchtime. As far as Grandpa
knew, they were in the doctor's waiting room.

Never in a million years could he have
imagined that they had in fact been imprisoned
by a madman in the basement of the library.

All traces of his love now wiped from his mind, Alfonso had immediately lost interest in Wanda, who kept sneezing away as she wiped her blonde hair on his shirt.

Now he was focused entirely on Sibylla.

He realised that he'd got his hopes up too soon. If he wanted to marry her, he'd have to catch her first – but that was not going to be easy.

To start with, he tried tempting her with kindness.

She's so young and innocent, he thought, *that she's sure to fall for my charms.*

'Come down here, little one,' he said in his sweetest voice. 'Come on, darling, and your Alfonso will give you a nice biscuit!'

Sibylla, laughing, pulled a lump of plaster from the ceiling and threw it at his head.

'Oww!' groaned Alfonso. 'So it's war you want, is it? Then so be it! Do you think you can escape me forever? I'll get you, you ugly witch, and I'll make you pay!'

And he started chasing after her, with his arms up in the air. Even though the ceiling was fairly low, Sibylla always just managed to dodge out of his way, darting into the opposite corner of the basement.

If I had a butterfly net, I'd catch her in no time, thought Alfonso, looking around to see if there was anything that might come in handy.

All he found was a stick, which he started swinging around in the air as if trying to hit a piñata.

'Stop that at once!' shouted Wanda. 'Can't you see you're going to hurt her? Aaachoo!'

She was absolutely furious, and she had no idea what her admirer (her *ex*-admirer, in actual fact, but she didn't know that yet) was up to.

What on earth . . . ? she wondered. First he'd paid Sibylla hardly any attention at all. He'd literally had his hands on her, but he'd dumped her inside an encyclopedia box. And now he was hunting her as if it were a matter of life and death. The man was crazy!

'Stop it!' she repeated. 'Leave my little sister alone! What are you trying to do to her?'

'I'm trying to catch her so I can marry her!' replied Alfonso, still waving the stick in the air.

'But didn't you want to marry me?' said Wanda in astonishment. *Men are so fickle!* she thought. 'Besides, haven't you noticed she's only a year old?'

It was like talking to a brick wall. The young man had completely taken leave of his senses and was racing around, bumping into the stacks of books – which tumbled down on to him in clouds of dust – tripping over his feet, swearing, falling down and getting back up again . . .

Suddenly there was a bang – and the basement was plunged into darkness.

Alfonso had managed to whack the only light bulb. It had smashed into smithereens.

Sibylla started wailing. She may have been a witch, but she was still a little girl who had only just learned to walk. She was sobbing and trembling, perched up high in the darkness like a little bat, when she heard a reassuring whisper right in her ear: 'Don't be afraid, mistress. Everything's going to be fine. We're here now.' And the gentle touch of a feather brushed her cheek.

At the same moment Alfonso let out a piercing shriek: five claws as sharp as needles had buried themselves in his calf.

'Shut-up! Mephisto! What are you doing here?' cried Wanda. 'Quick! Go and fetch someone to free us!'

To the Rescue

Zac, who was checking out the taps, with the old caretaker, saw a big bird fly in through the window, squawking, 'In the basement! In the basement! Danger! Help! Criminals!!!'

'You see? I was right,' said Zac. 'The problem with the plumbing is down in the basement. Someone must have sabotaged it. That's why there's no water.'

'Seriously?' replied the caretaker. 'Do you think I'm going to let a parrot tell me how to do my job?'

'Danger! Help! Criminals! Basement!' screeched Shut-up, flapping his wings in Zac's face.

'Danger? What's going on in the basement? Who's in danger?'

'Mistress, danger! Sibylla, Wanda. Help!'

'Sibylla? Wanda? So it's not the plumbing! Quick. Let's run!'

'Told you so,' muttered the caretaker, limping after him.

All's well that ends well.

The two rescuers burst into the basement and turned on the emergency lighting to see Alfonso Terribile buried under a mountain of books that the crafty Mephisto had knocked over to put him out of action. Luckily, like all cats, Mephisto could see in the dark.

Zac, immediately recognising Black Magic

Boy, picked him up off the floor, shook him, and when Wanda told him what had happened, he gave him a couple of slaps, while the caretaker limped off to call the police.

When the two policemen arrived, they put Alfonso in handcuffs and carted him off to prison.

And that's where he was, in prison, when his deadline came and went. Having failed to woo and wed a witch, Alfonso Terribile lost his inheritance of fifty million once and for all.

But let's get to the important moment: the opening of the envelope.

Inside the envelope was a note from Great-Uncle Sempronio:

'Excellent! Things have turned out exactly as I hoped. That idiot Alfonso has not passed the test. My fortune will therefore be divided into two

equal parts. Half will go to the witch who refused to marry my wet lettuce of a great-nephew, as a reward for her good sense and her lack of greed. The other half will go to the sole descendant of my dear Prunisinda, the grandson of her big brother Empedocle, who emigrated to Argentina in 1909.'

The solicitor sighed and scratched his head.

'Yet more problems!' he grumbled. 'It was Wanda who rejected Alfonso, but she's not a witch . . .'

'Sibylla rejected him too,' her sister objected. 'In fact, she gave him a good beating with the broom.'

And so the sum of twenty-five million was deposited at the bank in an account for the little witch.

Imagine their parents' surprise when they returned from England to find that their little baby was not only a witch, but also a multi-millionaire!

'And what about this heir? The wife's relative in Argentina?' said the solicitor. 'Now I'm going to have to scour the whole of Argentina to track him down.'

'You won't have to look that far,' said Diomira, who had accompanied Wanda to the opening of the envelope. 'Do you remember my poor sister Ermelinda, Zac's mother? When she died, she was a widow. But her husband came from Argentina. And her father-in-law's name was . . . Empedocle.'

'Zac's grandfather!' Wanda exclaimed happily. 'So our friend is Prunisinda's great-nephew! A witch's great-nephew . . . The world's such a small place!'

So the other half of the fifty million went to Zac, the sole heir of Sempronio Terribile's late wife.

And do you know what Zac did with the money? He expanded the library, bought new

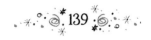

books, emptied the basement and restored all the antique books that had fallen upon the reckless Alfonso Terribile.

When the time came, he married Wanda.

But that was many, many years later – after she had graduated in xenoarchaeology and made lots of very important discoveries about extra-terrestrial prehistory.

Sibylla got married eventually too. Can you guess who to? Sigfrido Garlasconi, of all people. Yes, Wanda's old crush. They lived a life of luxury, travelling the world, not on a broomstick, but with Great-Uncle Sempronio's millions.

However, I must say that I think someone in this story has been treated unfairly.

After all, surely the mouse who nibbled the pages of the magic book deserves some kind of reward!

It was only because of that mouse that

Alfonso Terribile's information was incomplete and so he didn't notice Sibylla until it was too late. Instead – fate can be so cruel! – Zac's inheritance meant that the mouse suddenly found herself without any food down there in the basement, so she'd had to move into a bank instead, permanently changing the diet that she'd enjoyed ever since she was born. You can't tell me that banknotes have the same flavour and nutritional value as books.

And what exactly is the moral of this story? That there's no justice in the world for library mice!

Coming Soon!

Best Selling Author
BIANCA PITZORNO

Illustrated by
Quentin Blake

Lavinia
and the
Magic Ring

A funny, mischievous book about a girl who has an unexpected magic power that isn't for the squeamish.

One freezing Christmas Eve in Milan, seven-year-old Lavinia, a modern-day match girl, is alone and starving. Everyone is hurrying home to be with their families, and they have no time to help the little girl.

A fairy arrives in a taxi, and Lavinia gives her a match for free. The grateful fairy gives Lavinia a gift: a magic ring. Its special power? It allows the wearer to turn anything into poo – and back again. Lavinia is horrified and disgusted at first, but she soon works out how to use the ring to her advantage.

BIOGRAPHY

Bianca Pitzorno was born in Sardinia, but has lived and worked in Milan, Italy, since 1968. She studied Classics and, after a brief period as an archaeologist and a teacher, she worked for many years for Rai, the Italian national public broadcasting company, producing a large number of television shows for children. Her first book was published in 1970, and she has since written more than fifty books, which have been translated into many languages. In 1996, the University of Bologna granted her an honorary degree in educational science, and UNICEF made her a Goodwill Ambassador in 2001.